THE TRUE
ESSENCE OF EVIL

Book two
The Stories of Jo

Açil Pichon

Edited by R. Graves, K. Frank, and S. Slavinsky
Cover Photo by R. Graves & A. Pichon
Cover Design by Debbi Stocco

Printed in the United States of America
First Printing, 2016
ISBN: 978-0-692-49220-8 (print)

Acil Pichon Publishing
Louisiana
www.acilpichon.com

i

For every woman
who ever felt like a fool.

God My Father,
Thank you for blessing me with
insight and strength.
I know you give me exactly what I need in your
time; at the right time.
Your guidance means the world to me and I rely
on it each and every day.

Content

Introduction

In *Evil in Front of You*, book one of The Stories of Jo, Jo allowed herself to be surrounded by evil, which she'd suffered great consequence from. Her experience with Psycho wasn't the first time evil attacked Jo. She was actually surrounded by massive forces of evil for many years before Psycho ever entered her life.

Jo's twenty plus year relationship with her husband CJ was definitely something to reckon with. To the public, CJ and Jo's relationship looked rather healthy and peachy, but on the inside, Jo was slowly dying from CJ's manipulations and emotional abuse.

Like always, Satan used the things Jo was craving for the most to break her down. She wanted and fought for a healthy and loving marriage for her and her two daughters' sakes, but all the effort Jo put towards having a happy home and healthy marriage was never enough.

Unlike Psycho's demonic physical attacks, CJ's emotional and mental attacks on Jo were harder to recognize and defend, because CJ was a master when it came to being passive aggressive.

Evil is always right around the corner waiting to destroy. It camouflages itself to fit into your life where it is least noticed. Evil waits at the church alter for you, live under the same roof and share the same bed with you, be dependent on you, beg to be your friend, go on vacations with you, and even asks you to meet at Starbucks.

Evil is never far away, because it is always waiting to snatch hold of your life and soul to ruin. Where there is desperation, there is manipulation. There is also Evil doing everything in its power to keep you from moving on to bigger and better blessings.

Like many people, Jo didn't know the powers of Satan. It took several long years and extreme measures for Jo to realize that Satan is real, and her battles were spiritual battles.

The True Essence of Evil is a story that tells how Evil took control of Jo's life and mind for many years, and how it stood by laughing at Jo's weaknesses as it skated through life at her expense.

Chapter One
The Life

Jo grew up in Miser, Mississippi, which is a very small town where people thought they knew everything about everyone, and if they didn't, they would do whatever it took to find out. When they didn't really know the whole truth of someone's personal business, they'd make something up just to have a juicy piece of gossip to spread through the county.

Jo hated living in Miser, Mississippi more than anything else, because gossiping and backstabbing were people's favorite past times, and Jo wanted nothing to do with that. Jo always felt very much alone, because she didn't fit in anywhere or with anyone. It seemed no one there could or would think for themselves. Instead, they spent time judging everyone and giving horrible unwarranted advice. Jo could not wait to get out of Miser, so two weeks after her high school graduation, she got the hell out of there. She moved to New York City to attend an accredited interior design school.

While Jo was in school, she impressed most of her professors with her passionate work ethic, and she finished school at the top of her graduating class. Leaving school at the age of twenty-two with great recommendations from all of her professors, Jo was able to land a top job at one of New York City's most prestigious interior design firms. Jo had a job that every interior designer wished to have.

Living a city life in New York was a lot different and more fulfilling than the life she had in Miser. In New York Jo was just another person in the big city crown. She was a very

2

private person, so she loved that she could blend in and escape small town gossip.

When Jo finished college, her parents wanted her to move back home to get married and have children, but Jo wasn't having that. No way was she going to move back to Miser…Miserable, Mississippi.

Jo had no thoughts of leaving New York, because her life was very close to perfect there. She'd made more friends in New York in four years than she'd ever made in Miser in eighteen years. Jo was living the life. She lived in a very nice apartment in the upper east side of the city, and she felt very safe. She'd made friends with the doorman in her building, the lady at the Chinese restaurant where she ordered Yacht Mein soup from at least once a week, and the lady at the cleaners. She had a pet parrot, a big beautiful aquarium with a few fish, and she was more than just fine.

At the design firm, Jo had a large corner office with a nice view of the city, and her best friend Teresa worked in the firm as well. Most Thursdays and Saturdays Teresa and Jo would go out after work for happy hour, and sometimes they'd hit a night club or two.

Jo had freedom to do as she wished, was doing quite well financially for such a young lady, and her list of responsibilities included just a few important things that she didn't mind being responsible for.

Chapter Two
Endless Tears

Jo had never been a morning person, and one Tuesday morning in her high rise New York City apartment, she was awakened by the loud ringing of her landline telephone. "Hello." Jo answered with her deep sleepy morning voice.

"Jo," she could hear her mother speaking to her on the other end of the phone.

"Good morning Momma, Jo greeted with concern in her voice. "What's going on? Sounds like you are crying."

Jo's mother was crying, and she asked Jo if she would please move back to Mississippi.

Jo couldn't believe what her mother was asking her to do, because it was not a secret that Jo hated living in that small Mississippi town where it was hard to take a shit in private.

"Mom, you know I love you dearly, but you also know how much I've always hated living in Miser, and you would not be asking me to move back there unless it is something serious," said Jo. "What's going on Mom?" Jo asked.

"Jo, I've been diagnosed with Invasive Lobular Carcinoma," her mother said.

"Mom, calm down for a minute," Jo said in a calm soothing voice. "Whatever it is, I'm sure it'll be alright. Please tell me what Invasive Lobular Carcinoma is. You know I don't watch the news or much television at all, and that medical term is foreign language to me."

"It's breast cancer," Jo's mother answered. "And it's quite bad. I don't want anyone to know about it."

"Mom, that's nothing to be embarrassed about or to hide, and I really don't understand. You always get an annual mammogram," said Jo. "Why in the hell are they just now finding this out, and you're telling me it's pretty bad. What's the damn purpose of a mammogram?" Jo continued to fuss. "Damn doctors. Always inconveniencing people for this and that test, and they still don't know shit."

"Now YOU need to calm down Jo," her mother said. "Stop all that fussing and cursing."

"I apologize Mom. I just don't understand why this has to happen to you. Someone who always does what she supposed to do," said Jo.

"Listen to yourself!" Jo's mother said. "Just listen to you. Miss always have faith. Don't worry. God doesn't give us anything we can't handle. Do you remember saying all of those things?"

"Yes Mom, but," Jo said before her mother cut her off.

"But nothing Jo. I'm here, trying to be strong, but I'd feel much better if you were here with me. I know coming back here is the last thing you'd ever want to do, but," said Jo's mom.

"Say no more Mom," interjected Jo. "I don't want to be anywhere else at this time other than with you, so consider me there."

As much as Jo loved her life in New York City, she put in a two week notice at the design firm, called a packing and moving company, loaded up her car, and drove back to no personal or private space, no job, and no life. Jo cried the whole way back. There she was driving away from every little bit of a happy life and freedom she'd gained, back to Mississippi where she began to look for work in her field of study and her passion, interior decorating.

After going out every single day aggressively job hunting, Jo was still not able to find work in her field of choice. Unfortunately for her, there wasn't a demand for interior designers in Mississippi.

After unsuccessful job hunting each and every day, Jo went home, continued to assist her mother any way she could, and after, she'd flop down across the bed that she slept on as a kid, and cry until she cried herself to sleep.

Jo grew deeper and deeper into a state of depression, and she really didn't know what to do. There she was watching her mother suffer, and she missed her life and friends in New York.

Desperate for a job, Jo took work outside of her field of study as a delivery person for UPS. It wasn't what she wanted to do, but it did put money in her pocket and gave her a little break from the emotional struggles she was having from seeing her mom suffer each day battling with breast cancer.

As much as Jo wanted to be there for her mother every waking moment, she couldn't wait to move out of her parents' house, because her dad had been making her time in his house a living hell.

The day Jo went back to Mississippi and moved back into her parents' house was emotionally challenging. Even though she had a hefty savings and a degree under her belt, she felt like the biggest failure ever, and her dad didn't hesitate to make her feel that way day after day. There Jo was, moving backward instead of forward in life. She moved back to a place she vowed she would never return to.

Even though Jo was twenty-four years old, financially independent, and had been living on her own for a total of six years, her dad still treated her like an incompetent little teenager. Jo's dad did not allow her to go out, date, or receive phone calls from anyone. If Jo did receive a phone call, she had to take it in the living room where her parents would listen to every single word of her phone conversations. The few times Jo used the landline telephone located in her bedroom to make a call, her dad would pick up another phone in the house and listen in. Sometimes he'd pick up and sternly say, "Who the hell are you talking to? Get the hell off of my telephone."

That was most definitely embarrassing for Jo, and living back at home with her parents at the age of twenty-four was horrible. Jo had a very hard time adjusting to that new, but old way of living again. She'd lost the freedom she was so use to having when she lived in New York. There she was, taking care of her sick mother, wearing a brown uniform working on some crappy job not in her field of studies, living with a mean controlling father, no friends close by, no life, and depressed as ever. To top it all off, her extended family members didn't know the real reason why she'd moved back to Mississippi, so they ran around town telling everyone made up stories. Juicy lies and gossip that lacked accuracy. Jo hated hearing made up stories about her very own life, from people who didn't know a thing about her.

"Jo, I'm sorry you lost your job in New York," some would say. Others would say, "Jo, are you ok? I heard you moved back because you were sick."

Some of the things Jo would hear about herself left her speechless, but she wasn't one bit surprised because she didn't expect anything better than that from the people in Miser.

Jo moved back to Miser because she loved her mother very much and did not think twice about sacrificing whatever she had to sacrifice in order to be there for her mother. Believe it or not, caring for her mother was the

best part of Jo's days. Her mother needed her
and that's all that mattered at the time.

Chapter Three
Au Revoir Papa

The day Jo was able to pack her little belongings and move the hell out of her parents' house was an okay day for her. Not great, because she was still in Mississippi and wasn't as near as she'd like to be to her mother, but as good as it could ever be in that town. Jo found joy in getting her apartment together, because decorating and arranging furniture was something she was good at and loved doing.

As much as Jo hated working at UPS, she'd grown to like a few of her coworkers. They all took her in and treated her better than

14

her own extended family members did. When Jo's coworkers found out she was moving out of her parents' house and into her own little apartment, they all pitched in to help her move, and hosted a house warming party for her. Mr. Zimmerman gave Jo a table and four chairs for the breakfast area in her apartment, Mr. Douglass gave her some cooking and eating utensils, and Melissa gave her some glasses, pots, and dishes. There Jo was all settled in her very own apartment in what she called Miserable, Mississippi. She was glad to be out of her parents' house, away from her dad.

Moving out on her own and applying her skills to get her own little apartment together was a good sense of therapy for Jo. She was slowly but surely moving out of a very deep state of depression. Jo got out a little, and met a few potential friends.

One Sunday afternoon, Jo's mother called and asked her if she could go to the laundry mat to wash and dry her king size bed comforter. That was not a problem for Jo, because she found peace in helping her mother.

At the laundry mat, Jo sat and people watched while she waited for the bed comforter to wash and dry. People were coming and going, in and out. Hauling in and carrying out laundry baskets and bags. Putting clothes in and taking clothes out of washing machines and dryers. Jo just sat there and watched, as she reminisced about her life and friends in New York. She thought about all of the good fun they always had. She missed them so much. Jo also thought about her Florida friends that she was blessed to meet while working on a project in Ft. Lauderdale. She thought about how her Florida friends adopted her into their family, and showed her the ropes of living the beach life while she was there. Jo never felt as lost as she did that Sunday afternoon sitting in that uncomfortable laundry mat chair people watching.

As Jo sat there daydreaming, she didn't even notice when her cousin walked into the laundry mat. "Your mom told me I'd find you here," Tamara said. "I am cooking dinner this evening for Dad, and I'd like you to come by. I could use your help setting things up."

"I'll come there when I finish up here," replied Jo.

After finishing up at the laundry mat, returning the comforter and visiting with her mother, Jo went over to help Tamara set up for the special birthday dinner for her Uncle Charlie. After the dinner party was over, she helped with the clean up too. When Jo went outside to put trash in the garbage can, she saw who she assumed to be a friend of her uncle's walking up to the house. The dude looked very familiar to Jo. "How ya doin?" asked the stranger.

Jo nodded her head and gave the strange dude a little soft hello as she thought, "I've seen him somewhere before."

"Jo, I'd like you to meet my friend CJ. CJ Sims," said Jo's Uncle Charlie as he walked out of the house.

Turning to walk away, "Hi CJ," said Jo.

That night when Jo went back home, she could not stop thinking about CJ. It seemed like she'd known him from somewhere, or maybe seen him some place before. As much as she thought about it, she could never figure out where or how she knew CJ, but with Miser being such a small town, she was sure she'd seen him some place before.

Chapter Four
Dinner

Jo thought and thought, and finally she remembered where she'd seen CJ. She remembered seeing him as a child, loitering outside of the neighborhood convenience store with a bunch of hooligan boys. As a child Jo would be sitting in the car with her mother, while they waited for her dad to come out of the convenience store.

Just as her dad opened the car door to get in, he'd start fussing and cursing about those loud boys hanging outside of the pick-a-pack. Jo's dad would go on and on about how those boys were not supervised. "Where in the hell are their mommas?" he'd say. "That's what's wrong with kids these days. Running the damn streets, acting like a buncha wild animals, and their maws ain't no where around."

As Jo remembered, she imagined CJ the way he was back then, standing outside that convenience store with a smile on his face. She was even able to recall the feeling of interest she'd gotten every time she saw him as a child. Now seeing him as a man, that same feeling of interests appeared within her.

A few days after Jo's Uncle Charlie's birthday dinner, Tamara called Jo and told her that CJ asked about her. He wanted to know who she was and if she was dating anyone. Jo was flattered because she felt a deep urge to get to know CJ as well. For some strange reason the strong feeling of interest wouldn't go away.

Tamara asked her dad if he'd arrange for CJ to come over for dinner one night. "CJ would love to come over for dinner one evening. He loves your cooking Tamara. Just tell me when," Jo's Uncle Charlie said.

One Thursday evening after Jo got off of work, she went over to Tamara's house for dinner. When she walked into Tamara's house, there sat CJ on the couch talking to her Uncle Charlie. "Hello Uncle Charlie," greeted Jo, as she kissed him on his cheek, and looking towards CJ she nodded her head and said, "CJ."

"You didn't tell me CJ would be here. If I'd known, I would've gone home and changed out of this ugly brown UPS uniform," Jo said disappointedly.

"It's ok. You look just fine. It's not like CJ is a model for the GQ magazine or anything," said Tamara as she giggled. "If you hadn't noticed, he has on work boots."

CJ definitely was not a well-dressed man. He had on what looked like a pair of high water tie dye pants, military boots, an off the

21

wall striped shirt, and a purple bandana wrapped on his head with a knot in the back.

CJ, Uncle Charlie, Tamara, and Jo sat at the dining room table for dinner that night, and surprisingly, there was never a dull moment. CJ was full of Jokes, and he and Jo's Uncle Charlie told stories about their military days laughing nonstop. Jo's Uncle Charlie was CJ's sergeant and apparently CJ was a huge pain in the ass. After both men got out of the military, they reconnected and had been friends ever since.

A few times during dinner that evening, Jo laughed so hard at some of the stories CJ and Uncle Charlie were telling, she had to hold her mouth to stop food and water from flying across the table.

Dinner was great. Tamara's food was delicious as always and the company was extremely entertaining. After dinner when Jo began to collect and wash dishes, she recruited CJ to help. That would give them some time alone for small talk. During their conversation, Jo and CJ discovered that they grew up in the same church, knew a lot of the same people, and attended the same schools, but different years of course, because CJ was a few years older than Jo. They also discovered that their families frequented the same circles and knew of each other quite well. Not a huge coincidence, because Miser, Mississippi wasn't a large town at all, so it was pretty normal for people from the same cultural background to know one another.

Jo learned that CJ was the third child of four children and he grew up with no discipline or lessons what-so-ever. "I don't know who my daddy is," said CJ. "My momma had a lota men in and outa the house when I was young. My two olda sistas, Pam and Jackie have the same daddy, but my brotha Dale and I have different daddies than them. Basically, my ma got three baby daddies. One with my two olda sistas, one with me, and one with my baby brotha."

"Wow!" said Jo surprisingly.

"It's ok. No big deal," CJ said as he smiled so wide that his little to no lips disappeared. "I didn't have much of a motha either. She spent most of ha time workin at odd and end jobs, or hangin out drinkin in some barroom. My brotha and two sistas ain't nothin to brag about eitha. They gave a lot-a wild pardees and was always in some kinda trouble," said CJ. "I had my first drunk when I was five years old. My sistas and their friens kept givin me liqua, and they would say, 'drink, drink!' All I remember is puking my guts up while they stood and laughed at me. No one in my family care about me. Everybody fa themselves."

"That's quite sad," said Jo. "I'm sorry you had to grow up that way."

Chapter Five
Neglect

Jo felt pretty bad for CJ after learning about his childhood. Even though she thought she had a rough childhood growing up with a strict father, hers wasn't quite as bad as CJ's. At least she had a safe and secure roof over her head with parents who seemed to care. It's safe to say that Jo had a pretty normal childhood, but CJ didn't.

CJ and Jo began to see each other on a pretty regular basis, but it seemed like Jo wanted to spend time with CJ more than he wanted to spend time with her. CJ never called

Jo. She always had to call him or go over to his mother's house to see him and plan dates. It seemed he much preferred to hang with the guys.

CJ told Jo that he really liked her, but his actions showed something completely different. He never initiated visits or dates, and when they were together, he didn't treat her special at all, but that didn't stop Jo. Since CJ didn't grow up with many if any people caring about him, Jo was determined to show him what it was like to be cared for. She put forth as much effort as she could towards building a supportive and positive relationship with CJ, even though CJ didn't put forth any effort at all. Jo settled for the little to nothing CJ gave her.

Jo grew up in a chauvinistic family, so she knew what it was like to sacrifice and be put on the back burner. She grew up in a family where women had no value and were expected to cater to the men in their lives. A woman giving and not receiving was the way Jo saw relationships, and that's exactly what she was doing. Jo took whatever dirt and neglect CJ dished out to her, and she still continued to be nice to him. Emotional neglect wasn't something new to Jo, because that's how she was treated growing up; especially after her maternal grandfather took sick and died.

Jo had a very hard time understanding CJ, because he was horrible when it came to communication. He spoke broken English and used figurative language too much. When there was something CJ wanted to share, he quoted lyrics from songs by Sting. All CJ did was drink, smile like the Cheshire Cat, and make a bunch of unnecessary noise reciting unusual lyrics from songs.

Even though Jo continued to see CJ, she felt empty and sick to the stomach most of the time. She could feel in her gut something just wasn't right, but she was determined to help him become a better person by caring for him in a way his family never did, and Jo believed in giving more than receiving.

Jo was always sitting and waiting around for CJ. She waited for phone calls that she never received. Waited for him to ask her out, but he never did. Waited for him to drop by her apartment for a visit after work, but he never did. The few times CJ did drop by, it was late and he was drunk. Many weekends came and went, without one single call from CJ.

As Jo sat feeling rejected, she remembered the countless eligible and very successful bachelors she'd dated when she lived in New York. She thought about how her dates treated and respected her. They knew how to act like gentlemen, and she really missed that. Feeling pretty down, Jo decided to give Tamara a call.

"Tamara, have you or Uncle Charlie seen CJ lately?" asked Jo.

"No Jo. We haven't seen him in a while. Why?" asked Tamara. "I thought he's been with you."

"Not with me," said Jo. "I haven't seen him either. What in the hell am I doing sitting here allowing myself to be treated this way by a ditch digger Tamara? I deserve better than this. Here I am always waiting for CJ, and I get nothing. I'm tired of him," ranted Jo to Tamara.

Feeling impatient and unwanted, Jo decided to go on a date with Lonny.

Lonny was a very handsome guy who had been begging Jo to go out with him for several months. The few times Jo went to the one and only local hangout spot in Miser, she saw Lonny. He was a friend of Jo's high school associates, and he wasn't from Miser. That was the first thing Jo liked about Lonny. He was extremely easy on the eyes, and didn't have a problem letting Jo know he was interested and wanted to spend some time with her. Lonny

asked Jo out several times before, but she
always declined, because she was always
hoping to spend time with CJ, only to have him
stand her up like he always did.

Chapter Six
Choose

    Lonny and Jo's first date lead to a second date, a third date, and on and on. Not long after Jo began dating Lonny, he took her to meet his family. His family was very happy to meet Jo, and unlike CJ's family, they all welcomed her with open arms.

    Jo met and had been seeing CJ for well over six months, and he still did not formally introduce her to his family members. On the other hand, Jo and CJ did see his mother and siblings several times in the passing, but not even once did CJ take one moment to say, "This is my friend Jo."

Lonny lived an hour and a half away from Jo, and he had no problem driving a round trip to pick her up. One evening Lonny and Jo were going on what seemed to be their tenth date. Lonny had to pick Jo up from her parents' house that evening, because Jo had been spending a lot more time there since her mother started getting treatments more often. Knowing how strict and mean her dad was, Jo told Lonny that she'd check for him around eight o'clock and run out and meet him. "Do not get out of your car and knock on my parents' door. I'll come out to meet you," explained Jo to Lonny.

"Ok. I understand," said Lonny.

While Jo was in the bathroom at her parents' house, Jo heard her mother say, "Hi---Jo, Lonny is here to get you."

"What the hell!" thought Jo. "I told him to stay outside," as she hurried to finish dressing so she could get Lonny out of her parents' house and away from her dad in a quick but smooth manner.

As Jo dressed in a hurry, she heard a lot of loud talking and laughter coming from her parents' family room. When she finally went in there, Lonny greeted her with a nice hug and kiss on the lips. As much as Jo needed that hug and kiss, she felt a bit awkward and embarrassed, because her parents were there observing. "I'm' ready; we can go now," Jo said to Lonny.

Lonny walked over to Jo's mother and gave her a big kiss on her cheek and a big bear hug. "It's nice meeting you Mrs. James," Lonny said to her mother.

After, Lonny reached his hand out to meet Jo's father's hand for a handshake. "You're welcome to come here anytime, Man," Jo's father said as he shook Lonny's hand. "Have a good time Jo, and ya'll be safe."

"What just happened in there?" Jo asked Lonny. "I asked you to stay outside. And my dad has never been nice to anyone the way he was to you."

"I'm sorry Jo, but your dad is a real cool cat. And your mother is the cutest and nicest little woman ever," Lonny said. "I don't know why you didn't want me to meet them."

"Well, you've met them now, and it really doesn't matter anymore," said Jo in a matter of fact manner.

Over that weekend, Jo had a wonderful time with Lonny and his family. Lonny's mother and auntie prepared many special and delicious dishes just for Jo. They all treated Jo like family, but even during all of that, Jo could not stop thinking about CJ.

As soon as Lonny dropped Jo off at home that Sunday night, Jo hopped into her car and drove over to CJ's mother's house where CJ was living. To Jo's disbelief, CJ was actually home and sober. When CJ saw Jo walk into the door, he jumped up, hugged her tighter than he ever had before, and he wouldn't let her go. "I'm mad about you," said CJ to Jo.

"What?" asked Jo.

"I'm mad about you," he repeated.

Jo didn't bother to ask CJ what that meant. She was pretty sure it was some lyrics from one of them weird soulless songs he always listened to.

As much as CJ's actions showed he may have missed Jo, he never bothered to contact her over the weekend in any way.

Jo called Tamara to tell her about CJ's actions. "He called dad this weekend Jo, and asked him if he'd seen you, and dad told him no. When Dad got off of the phone with CJ, he asked me if I'd heard from you," said Tamara.

"And what did you tell Uncle Charlie?" asked Jo.

"When I told Dad I hadn't heard from you all weekend, he told me CJ hadn't heard from you either," said Tamara. "Then dad said, 'Sound like that boy might be missing Jo,'" Tamara laughed.

"CJ doesn't care about me Tamara. If he does, why doesn't he act like it?" Jo asked Tamara.

"Jo," said Tamara. "Most men like to hunt. They like the chase. I think you were too nice to CJ and you were always readily available. The moment you backed off, he changed his attitude. See, he knows how much you care about him, and he was taking you for granted. The moment he thought he lost you, he didn't know what to do with himself."

CJ confused Jo, and she really didn't know what to think of him.

A few days after Jo's weekend with Lonny and his family, Jo went over to her parents' house to meet with the nurse that had been helping to take care of her mother. Jo and her dad sat and ate dinner together. While they were having dinner, Jo's daddy said, "I really like that guy Lonny."

"I like him too Dad," responded Jo.

"I heard you've been dating somebody from across the tracks," stated Jo's father in a disapproving manner. "Is that true? Are you really seeing one of them niggas?" he asked.

"Yes, Dad," Jo answered.

"You can't see two different men at the same time Jo; so you need to choose," said her dad. "Decide which one you want to see. I really like Lonny. He's a nice respectable young man. Seems like somebody who wants something out of life. You need to leave that nigga from across the tracks alone. Ain't nothing good from over there anyway. You gotta decide. Which one do you love?"

Jo had never thought about love. She wasn't really sure if she knew exactly what love was, but she did know she thought a lot about CJ.

"I love the nigga from across the tracks," answered Jo.

When Lonny called to take Jo out the following weekend, she went. She really enjoyed Lonny's company and she was blown away by how much he reached out to her and actually wanted to be in her presence every free moment he had. Lonny was a perfect gentleman. On the other hand, Jo thought a lot about CJ, and she didn't think it was fair to Lonny. For some unknown reason, she wanted to be with CJ as much as Lonny wanted to be with her. She thought about what her dad told her, and he was right. Jo had to make a choice, because she didn't want to hurt Lonny. He was too good of a man.

"Tamara," said Jo. "Dad told me I need to choose between Lonny and CJ. Which one should I choose?" asked Jo.

"Jo, that's up to you. I can't tell you what to do. Which one makes you feel good?"

"I enjoy my time with Lonny a lot. It feels good to be wanted. But what should I do?" asked Jo.

"Be with the person you want," replied Tamara.

After a lot of thought, Jo thought it was best to let Lonny go. Even if she didn't end up with CJ, it was not fair to waste Lonny's time or lead him on.

One evening after work Jo drove over to Lonny's house to sit and have a talk with him. She told Lonny about dating him and seeing CJ at the same time. "I don't want to continue to do that," said Jo. "It's not fair to you."

"Thank you Jo," said Lonny. "I appreciate your honesty. I'm not here to hold you back in anyway. If you feel you want more than I can give you, by all means go after it. If you change your mind, you know where to find me, because I'll always care for you."

Jo and Lonny exchanged a close intimate hug, and said their final goodbyes.

With CJ being inconsistent and extremely inconsiderate, Jo was rightly unsure about her decision, but she felt she was following her heart.

Chapter Seven
Better Than That

Unfortunately for Jo, CJ never changed. He continued to hang in the run-down neighborhood barroom each evening after work. He'd drink himself to a drunken stupor, and go home to his momma's house where she had a few split fried chicken legs waiting on him. CJ would scoff down fried chicken drumsticks in a starving manner, and pass out on one of the two sofas in his momma's living room where he slept most nights.

From the left side of CJ's mouth he'd tell Jo, "I'm mad about you," and from the right side of his mouth he'd ask, "Who are you and what are you doing here?" as if he had never seen her before. Many times Jo and CJ would make plans to meet up, but CJ would never show up. At times it was like CJ was running from Jo, and when Jo backed off, he seemed hurt and acted as though he missed her.

One Saturday evening Jo and Tamara went to pick up CJ from his mother's house to go to a party. While they were there, the telephone rang. With CJ's permission, Jo answered. "Hello," she greeted.

"Is CJ home?" a female's voice on the other end of the phone asked.

"Hold on," Jo said before handing the phone to CJ.

CJ sat there in front of Jo and Tamara talking to another woman with a shit eating grin on his face. Jo could tell that the woman on the other end of the telephone asked CJ about her. "My girlfrien. Naw! No not really. I guess.

Somethin like that," CJ explained into the phone
as he laughed like a junior high school boy
caught kissing another girl.

After the phone call ended, Jo
questioned CJ, and all he did was laugh. He
didn't say anything to make Jo feel better about
what she and Tamara heard and saw going on.
Jo was very hurt, so she politely stood up from
sitting on his momma's couch, walked towards
the door, and left. Tamara followed Jo out of
the door and insured her of what they'd just
witnessed.

"Jo, CJ was talking on the phone with
another woman and he denied having any type
of relationship with you," said Tamara.

"I know. I was there too, remember?"
said Jo in such a letdown state.

Jo was a glutton for punishment, because
she continued to go back to CJ, and he
continued to act the same as he always did. He
went to work most days when he wasn't too

43

drunk to go in, and after work he hung out at the neighborhood barroom with his buddies, over indulging in alcohol beverages.   When he could barely stand up, he'd leave and go home to his momma's to eat the fried chicken legs she always left out for him, and pass out on the couch as always. As that cycle continued, Jo was still there waiting around for him to change.

Jo's coworker and family friend Ms. Melissa was older than Jo's parents and she was more like a wise godmother figure to Jo. Ms. Melissa was also from CJ's neighborhood across the tracks, so she knew all too well about the low downs from around there. After Jo started seeing CJ, Ms. Melissa could clearly see Jo's minimal self-esteem diminishing to nothing. "What is wrong with you Jo?" Ms. Melissa asked. "Is your self-esteem that damn low?"

"What do you mean?" Jo asked.

"Jo, do you not have standards where guys are concerned?" asked Ms. Melissa. "You keep waiting around for that boy to change. He's never gonna change. Look at his family. His momma, sisters, AND brother. All of them ain't shit Jo. I see CJ's ass hanging by that barroom every evening, getting drunk with all the rest of the low lives from across there. You'll never change him, so you should move on. I know your mom and dad, and they raised you better than that," said Ms. Melissa.

"I don't even know the guy Jo," chimed in Jo's other coworker, Mr. Zimmerman. "But I do know he doesn't make you happy. I've seen you come in here upset too many mornings since you've been seeing him. There really isn't any reason why an independent and very pretty young lady such as yourself settle for someone like that."

As Ms. Melissa and Mr. Zimmerman stood there stating their opinions to Jo, she heard them, and was trying to process everything they said to her. Jo grew up hearing all sorts of negative things about herself from family members, so hearing them say good, positive things about her didn't really register.

"You stupid motha-fucka," is something Jo had grown accustomed to hearing. Along with, "You're not smart enough to do that." or "You're not pretty enough."

Even though Jo proved what people in her family said about her to be wrong, by graduating at the top of her class, working for the most prestigious design firm, and living a top shelf life in New York City, she could still hear them saying those ugly things to and about her. "Maybe I do have a low self-esteem," Jo said to Ms. Melissa.

Jo subconsciously believed every negative thing she heard about herself growing up, and there she was, back in Mississippi. A place she'd vowed to never return to.

"Who am I to deserve better?" Jo thought.

Chapter Eight
Best Friend

Sitting at home alone one evening, Jo reminisced about her old best friend Julie. Julie was a few years older than her, and they worked together side by side during Jo's high school days. Even though Jo had many friends in New York, she never had a best friend like Julie.

During Jo's junior and senior year in high school, she was a manager at a party supply store where Julie was the regional manager and her boss. Jo and Julie had a great working relationship, and in time, a well-respected friendship bloomed between the two.

Anytime they had some time off of work together, they hung out with each other. Jo and Julie were like two peas in a pod. Julie was twenty one years old and Jo was only seventeen at that time, but that didn't make a bit of difference. The two young ladies were always able to relate to one another and the support between the two was a type of support that was very hard to come by in Miser. Even though Julie and Jo were still very much so young, they were more responsible and had more financial freedom than most women in Miser.

One day Jo and Julie met for lunch, and during their conversation, they realized they had been working without many days off. After sharing how tired and overworked they both felt, the two ladies decided a vacation was long overdue. Neither one of them had ever flown in an airplane before, so they went to the one and only travel agency in Miser, and purchased two round trip plane tickets to go to Atlanta, Georgia for an extra-long weekend.

Even though Jo's dad was very strict and didn't want her to have any social life what-so-ever, he did allow her to work and participate in work events. In order for Jo to use the plane ticket she purchased to go to Atlanta, she had to lie to her parents. She told them she and Julie were flying to Georgia for a job training. The lie was easily believable, so Jo and Julie had a memorable time in Atlanta, Georgia. Jo even went to a nightclub for the first time in her life, at the age of seventeen.

Another time back in those days, Jo and Julie wanted to see what it was like to be drunk.

"Have you ever been drunk before?" Julie asked Jo.

"No," answered Jo, "Why?"

"Well I have never been drunk before either, so I want to see what it's like," replied Julie.

"I don't like the taste of alcohol," said Jo, "so I really don't know about that."

"We'll get something you like. Come on, let's do it. Let's get drunk together," said Julie, full of excitement.

"Ok," agreed Jo.

After work that night, Jo and Julie went to the one and only liquor store on the service road in Miser, and loaded up their trunks with every kind of alcohol in that store. Julie and Jo's car trunks were loaded with enough alcohol to supply a barroom for a month. They drove out to the marina near the church where Jo's daddy's boat was docked, sat on the edge of the bayou and had a tasting session of all the different alcohol beverages they'd purchased. Once Jo narrowed down to one that she liked, she drank and drank and drank strawberry Boones Farm until she couldn't drink anymore.

Thinking about her and Julie's friendship brought back some good and hilarious memories, so Jo decided to give Julie a call.

"Hello Julie," said Jo. "Remember me?"

"JO! Is that you?" asked Julie. "I miss you so much. We have so much to catch up on. Come over."

At Julie's house, the two sat and caught up on life. During their conversation, Jo told Julie about seeing CJ. "CJ?" Julie asked smiling. "We are so much alike, because I've been talking to a guy named CJ too. I just met him two weeks ago."

Jo's radar spiked up with instant concern. Her stomach had a knot, she could feel her blood pressure rising, and the saliva in her mouth increased.

"I hang out at the neighborhood barroom across the tracks a few times a week shooting pool," Julie told Jo, "and that's where I met CJ."

"I think your CJ is my CJ," said Jo.

"No Jo. Can't be. I told you I met CJ at The Swamp Shack across the tracks, and you don't go to places like that."

"Julie, the CJ I've been seeing hangs out at that same place," replied Jo. "There isn't very many guys with the name CJ who hangs out at that barroom across the tracks."

"Jo, it's just a coincidence," said Julie.

"Bullshit!" snapped Jo. "There is just one CJ who hangs at The Swamp Shack across the tracks. Call him now!"

Julie got CJ on the phone, and Jo listened to the conversation on the other line. Jo heard CJ talk to Julie in a way that he'd never spoken to her before.

"You mean he knows how to ask a girl out," Jo thought, as she listened to CJ beg Julie to meet him out later that night.

In the middle of Julie and CJ's phone conversation, Jo got fed up and couldn't take it anymore.

"How are you doing today, CJ?" Jo chimed in from the other line.

"Julie?" asked CJ.

"No! JO!" said Jo.

"Wait, wait. Who I'm talking to?" CJ asked, confused.

"Well you were talking to Julie, but now you are talking to me, Jo," answered Jo in a very calm, but smart ass way.

CJ grew angry and started shouting at Julie.

"WHAT DA HELL YOU DONE? WHY YOU DO DIS TO ME? Jo! Jo! Talk to me!"

Jo hung up the phone, left Julie's house and went home. Shortly after she made it to her apartment, CJ showed up knocking on her door, but Jo refused to let him in. He stood at her door pleading his case. He begged Jo to forgive him, but she wouldn't give in. Not until he said, "I don't like that girl Jo. She's white trash. All I wanted her to do was suck my dick."

Oral sex wasn't something Jo did, because she didn't see any love at all in that type of sexual behavior, so to her, CJ didn't love her friend Julie. She told herself all CJ wanted from Julie was sex.

"Here he is begging me to forgive him," Jo thought, "so that counts for something."

With reluctance, Jo allowed CJ to enter her apartment, but she felt sick to her stomach every time she looked at him. She really didn't know what to think or do. Anger from CJ's cheating had taken over her, but another part of her felt wanted, because CJ ran over to plead his case and beg for her forgiveness.

"Apparently, oral sex is something only white trashy women do, so don't you EVER expect me to suck your dick," said Jo to CJ.

Chapter Nine
Dirty

CJ continued to put Jo through hell. He did all sorts of things to Jo, and as always, she made excuses for his horrible behavior, forgave him, and continued to see him. Hearing CJ talk down about her to another woman on the phone wasn't enough to make Jo leave him. Meeting and having sex with trashy women, as CJ said, wasn't enough to make Jo leave him. Getting stood up and dealing with his drunkenness wasn't enough to open Jo's eyes and get her attention either.

CJ did some low down dirty things to Jo, and when she asked him about them, he'd laugh and call her crazy, or play dumb and innocent as if he didn't know his actions were inappropriate.

Even though Jo knew exactly what was really going on because she witnessed a lot first hand, CJ had a way of making Jo second guess herself. There were times when she thought she was crazy or losing her mind, because CJ would convince her that what really happened didn't happen. He'd tell her she was seeing or hearing things, and misunderstood the intentions behind his or his family's heinous actions.

Jo knew what she saw and heard, but being the loved starved and optimistic person she was, she'd push those things out of her mind, and keep on kicking.

One Friday after work Jo went over to pick CJ up for an early dinner. Every time she went over to that house and stepped out of her car, she had to hold her breath not to smell the stink in the yard. CJ had a dog around there that he called CJ, just like himself. Every dog he ever owned was called CJ, which was short for his very own name, Calvin Joseph. That dog was so stink it smelled like it was dying from the inside out. Jo was willing to bet that dog never had a bath a day in its life. She felt sorry for the dog, because it was quite obvious that the dog was greatly neglected.

"I'm not the only thing CJ neglects," thought Jo.

When Jo made it into the house, there CJ sat on one of the two sofas in his mother's very small living room. He sat with his usually wide thin to no lip smile on his face. A smile as big as the Jokers.

Jo walked two steps over to the couch and sat down next to CJ.

"What's going on?" she asked.

CJ reached into his shirt pocket and pulled out a prescription bottle of pills to show Jo.

"The people from da health unit called me yesterday. Tole me I needed to come in and get tested for a STD. Dat ol girl had a disease and turned my name in cuz she had sex with me. I gotta take these pills."

As CJ sat there with those words coming out of his mouth, he continued to smile and actually laugh as if that shit was funny. Jo sat there looking at him as the stupid person he was.

"What is so damn funny?" she asked.

"Them people say I got some kinda disease," said CJ as he continued to laugh.

"You have to take pills because you have a sexually transmitted disease, and here you sit smiling and laughing," said Jo, as she shook her head. "What girl have you been with?"

"It doesn't matter. My brotha was wit ha too, and the same thing happen to um," said CJ.

"You and your brother had sex with the same girl?" asked Jo. "What kind of people are you?"

"I'll be a'ight afta I take these pills," said CJ.

Jo thought shit like that only happened in the movies. What CJ told her was sick and shocking, and all she could do was sit there and shake her head in disgust. But that didn't stop her. Jo continued to see CJ and attempt to transform him. The hold he had on her was indescribable.

CJ's sisters thought he was as good as gold and deserved the best. His younger sister Jackie had the audacity to tell Jo how lucky she was to have CJ.

"You his one and only ol lady," Jackie told Jo. "You think he eva broght a-notha girl here befo?"

Even though Jo knew much more about CJ than his sister ever would, she didn't tell her any better, because she was his sister after all. Instead, Jo looked at the way CJ's younger sister carried herself and quickly figured out the fact that she had no clue about life or anything for that matter, and couldn't even try to get a clue because she didn't have enough sense to try.

When Jo told Tamara about CJ having a sexually transmitted disease and the things his younger sister told her, Tamara immediately grew angry.

"Be glad you ain't started having sex with him yet. Are you telling me his sister told you that?" asked Tamara.

"Yes, his younger sister, Jackie," answered Jo.

"Is that the one who drives around town in that ol beat up green car that got da paint peelin off? The one who pick up CJ mom Ms. Sims from workin at da truck stop almost every day?" asked Tamara.

"YES Tamara, that one!" answered Jo. "Jackie."

"That dope smokin pill poppin alcoholic has no fuckin clue," Tamara said angrily. "CJ is an undercover man ho. Of course he don't bring them things around his family. If the Sims were my family, I wouldn't bring people around them fuckers either," laughed Tamara. "Besides, any man with a little damn sense knows not to bring their ho-of-the-week or booty-call-of- the-night around ANYBODY," Tamara continued to rant full of frustration. "Most of them hoes him and his brother fuckin are strawberries or blueberries anyway."

"What's a blueberry?" Jo asked.

"Jo, you do know what a strawberry is right?" asked Tamara.

"Yes Tamara. Isn't a strawberry a woman who trades sex for drugs?" asked Jo.

"Yeah, Jo, but you still don't get an A in street life," Tamara said as she laughed. "If ya want an A, tell me what a blueberry is."

"Hell! I don't know! That's why I asked you," replied Jo, laughing.

"Well, brace yourself Jo. A BLUEBERRY is what people on da streets call A MAN who trade sex for drugs," Tamara said with an expectancy look on her face waiting to see Jo's response.

"Jo, I hope you know CJ's brother IS the drug lord across dem tracks. Why ya think all dem crack head men and women, or strawberries AND blueberries be back there by CJ momma house where all their trifling asses live? And what kinda momma is she to KNOW her son sell drugs and have him in her house?"

63

"Tamara, stop it!" said Jo. "I don't even think about all that, and you know I don't like hearing all that dirty laundry."

Chapter Ten
Milk for Free

One weekday evening CJ showed up at Jo's apartment mad and flustered.

"I can't keep livin back there in my momma house Jo," CJ said in a blunt and desperate way.

"Today my younga crack head sista Jackie came home and said somethin stupid like she always do. Made my brotha Dale click. He beat ha ass like-a man," CJ said, fighting to hold back tears of disgust.

"I couldn't take dat shit, so I went in da room where he was, drug him outa bed and beat his ass like he beat ha. My dumb ass momma stood there cryin fa me to stop even afta he beat ha own daughta up. HOW DARE I beat up ha favorite son? It's BAD ova there Jo."

Jo didn't know what to say. That was some crazy shit and she was not used to dealing with or being around people or drama like that.

"DAMN! I'm sorry that happened," she said to CJ.

"Yo family ain't nothin like mine. You lucky cuz you grew up wid-a daddy. I'm jealous of you," said CJ.

"That's the most foolish thing I have ever heard," said Jo. "How can anyone be jealous of me?"

"You know who yo daddy is. I ain't have no daddy. Hell! No momma eitha, and my brotha and sistas got problems," said CJ. "Ya know about my brotha selling dope, runnin with hoes and beatin his wife," said CJ.

"I know about you running with whores too," Jo thought without saying it, because it wasn't the right time.

"And Jackie, my younga sista is da evilest and biggest hypocrite I know. She da first thing knockin down the church doe," CJ went on.

"My olda sista Pam is a crack head. Hit da pipe and put powda up ha nose. Drunk all da time. Been with every man in the neighborhood. Even the married ones. She's in everybody's business. Writin and sendin anonymous threatenin lettas to my brotha baby momma and family. She even sent one to a girl I was with. She get full of ha shit, start slurring like a sloppy drug head and drunk, and don't know how to keep ha damn mouth shut. I feel sorry fa her daughta. Pam get so damn drunk, and passes out. My lil niece stands ova ha crying, 'Mommy, get up,' and ha ass be too damn drunk to wake up fa ha own daughta," CJ said.

Jo just sat there and listened as CJ continued to go on and on venting about his horrible family. She found herself feeling sorry for him and at that moment, she began to make excuses for his behavior. She realized CJ was a product of his environment and he didn't know any better because he had never been taught any better.

"Jo, you just don't know how bad my family is and da things they put me through," CJ continued.

"I do have an idea," replied Jo.

"As much as my olda sista stay in eerbody business, she neeta learn hotta mine ha own. Bill collectas callin me cuz she owe dem money. And yestaday, a finance company called becuz she foe months behind on her little travel traila note. Stupid bitch have her priorities backwards, and always in somebody else business. My sistas so fucked up, they can't get a man. Nobody wont em. Dey sloppy as hell, and have no kinda self-respect or decency. Dey all fucked up Jo, and I wouldn't deal with 'em if I didn't hafta."

Jo just sat and listened as CJ continued to go on and on about his horrible family.

"Jo, I'm tide of all dat, and I'm tida sleepin on my momma couch. Can I move in wicha?"

Jo wanted to help CJ out, but she didn't believe in shacking up with a man.

"If you can get the milk free, why buy the cow," Jo said to CJ.

"I don't understand what ya sayin Jo," said CJ.

"My mother told me to never live with a man or allow a man to live with me before marriage. She says, 'If you can get the milk free, why buy the cow.' I can't allow you to live with me CJ. It goes against my beliefs and what my mother taught me," said Jo.

"Oh, I get it na," said CJ. "We don't hafta sleep in da same bed. I'll sleep in da otha room."

After great thought, Jo decided to allow CJ to move in with her. She didn't want to see CJ get caught up in a drug bust back there at his momma's. CJ was a lot of not so good things, but a drug dealer he wasn't. Plus with CJ's financial contribution towards the rent, she'd be able to help her parents out a little more.

Jo didn't tell her parents about CJ being her new roommate, but they found out anyway. One night her dad dropped by for a visit and saw CJ was there and very much at home.

"So you two are living together now?" Jo's dad asked. "When do you two plan to get married?"

The only time Jo ever thought about marriage was when her dad brought it up.

Every time he went over for a visit, marriage was the topic of discussion. Jo's dad would not let the subject rest. "You two are living together now. It's time for you to get married," he'd always say.

Because of the pressure from her dad, and the guilt she carried around from 'shacking up' like the people in Mississippi would say, Jo and CJ started to talk about and plan to marry. He promised Jo he would change for the better, and she was hopeful that he would.

When Miser locals heard about Jo planning to marry CJ, they made many concerned remarks.

"You're marrying that Sims boy? Isn't he a drug dealer? " People would ask Jo. "Be careful honey. I hear that Sims family is some-thin else."

"I'm not marrying THAT Sims boy." Jo defended herself. "I'm marrying the older of the two boys; the good one," trying to convince

71

herself at the same time that CJ was better than his family and not what he'd shown himself to be.

"I neva thought dat boy would ev-a settle down," said an older lady from CJ's neighborhood who'd known him all of his life. "I see him hangin out by that Swamp Shack. Maybe you kin straighten him out some Honey."

Chapter Eleven
Message Ignored

After many long months of planning, the wedding day was finally there. Jo woke up with a sick stomach that morning, and she made several trips to the bathroom to hug the toilet. Jo could not keep anything down in her stomach that morning. Not even water. And even though she was feeling very sick, she still managed to get things done that day. She finalized deliveries and even made it through a photo shoot.

By the afternoon, after upchucking everything inside of her, the queasiness in her stomach subsided some.

On Jo's ride to the church for her wedding that Saturday night, she didn't talk much at all while she looked out of the limousine window. As the limousine approached the church, Jo saw a lot of cars in the parking lot ahead, and at that precise moment, reality hit her and the queasiness reappeared in her stomach like a ton of bricks. The feeling was worse than ever; extremely uncomfortable and persistent at the same time. The power of that feeling brought tears to Jo's eyes.

"What's wrong?" Tamara, Jo's maid of honor asked.

Tears slowly fell from Jo's eyes, and she didn't speak a word.

"What's wrong Jo?" Tamara asked again. "Ya'll, she's crying," said Tamara to Jo's parents.

"It's too late for that now," barked Jo's mother.

Just as the driver announced their arrival at the church, the limousine door opened, and there stood Jo's wedding planner. When the wedding planner noticed the tears coming from Jo's eyes, she patted them dry and coached her to getting herself together.

"Let's dry your eyes and get ready Honey," said the wedding planner. "The priest and your groom are waiting for you. Stand there and let me straighten out your beautiful cathedral train and veil."

Before Jo could blink, she was already married to CJ and walking out of the church. The longer than sixty minute catholic ceremony seemed to fly by very fast, and CJ couldn't run out of the church fast enough to get to the wedding reception where there was an open bar serving premium bar brands.

The wedding reception was just as much a blur to Jo as the ceremony. Jo did not feel like a happy bride at all. She walked around alone most of the night greeting more than three hundred wedding guests in which she didn't know most of them. Jo could not wait to get out of there, and away from all of the craziness that was going on. She needed some time alone. Something she hadn't had in a very long time.

CJ barely spent five minutes with Jo that entire night. She could only remember seeing him for a total of three minutes and twenty two seconds when they danced their first dance, in which CJ made a mockery of because he had no idea how to hold Jo during a slow dance.

When it was time for the bride and groom to leave the reception and head off for their honeymoon, CJ's younger crack head sister followed behind Jo and kept whispering in her ears, "Open ya mout. It's justa lil piece-a paper. It'll help ya enjoy yo night."

"No thank you Jackie," said Jo. "I don't do drugs."

"Awe com-on girl. You won't feel a thing. Open yo mout," Jackie kept insisting.

Jo despised drugs and drug users, so she had sense enough not to fall for that foolishness.

Besides fighting the peer pressure of CJ's horrible sister, Jo still had that horrible knot in her stomach from the beginning of the night.

There she was, married to a man who could care less about her, and she was expected to have sex with him that night as his wife. The more Jo thought about what she was expected to do at the end of the night, the bigger that knot in her stomach grew, and as much as Jo despised CJ's drinking and over indulgence in alcoholic beverages, she hoped he'd get wasted that night so she didn't have to have sex with him.

Chapter Twelve
Gossip Hounds

Jo made some delicious lemonade out of lemons. Even though she was unhappily married to CJ, she woke up each and every single day with a huge smile on her face. Being married to CJ was a huge task, and his way of living made life harder and harder for Jo. Instead of gaining a husband, Jo felt like she'd gained an oversized kid with no common sense. It was easy to detect that CJ did not have what most people call a normal upbringing, and it was obvious that he had a severe case of Attention Deficit Hyperactivity Disorder topped with a huge drinking problem. Instead of marrying a man, Jo married a problem. And on top of that problem she inherited four others; CJ's mother and his three siblings.

About four months after the wedding when Jo was at work, one of many people in Miser who liked to squash other people's happiness stomped on Jo's fake happiness in a blink of an eye. Jo was in the middle of an innocent conversation with her coworker Tilly.

"I heard about your in-laws not wanting CJ to marry you," Tilly said.

That was news to Jo. She was shocked.

"This is the first I'm hearing of that," said Jo. "I didn't know they didn't want CJ to marry me."

"Oh yeah girl," replied Tilly excitedly. "CJ's cousin Ken and I are very close, and a few nights befo ya'll wedding, Ken came to my house. We sat on the porch, and he told me all about CJ's family not wanting CJ to marry you."

"If they didn't want CJ to marry me, why did they participate in our wedding? They stood by our sides in the church. Both of his sisters and his brother too. They were my bridesmaids and his brother was his best man," Jo said feeling like she had to defend herself.

"You know them people," said Tilly. "Them Sims will do anything for attention. Even standing up by your side for a wedding they didn't want to happen."

After listening to everything Tilly told her, Jo's feelings were hurt. When she went home that evening after work, she shared Tilly's conversation with CJ. Defending his family like he always did, CJ said, "That ain't true. You can't believe everything you hear."

Jo was a bit confused and didn't know what to believe. All she could think about was the fact that CJ's cousin Ken wasn't a known liar, and he seemed to be a compassionate person who wouldn't make up bad things about anyone. When Ken spoke to Tilly about conversations he'd heard CJ's sisters having, he quoted their statements word for word, and reported exactly which family member said what. Ken couldn't have made up those ugly things he'd reported, and when Jo told CJ that, CJ told Jo she was over reacting.

"You always misunderstand stuff, and you can't believe what Tilly say. She messy!" said CJ.

"Tilly may be messy CJ, but your people don't have a very good track record themselves, and you know it," said Jo.

As Jo lay in bed next to her husband that same night, her mind wouldn't stop wondering. She wondered why CJ's family would say such ugly things about her. She never did any of them anything, and they all seemed excited during the wedding events. Why would his sisters and brother stand next to her and CJ when they said their vows if they didn't agree with the union?

"Oh my God! Those tears they cried during the wedding ceremony weren't tears of joy; they were tears of pain. They were crying because they didn't want CJ to marry me," Jo thought, as her self-esteem decreased even more.

Approximately a week after Tilly's gossiping session to Jo, Jo received a phone call at work from Dakota, her brother-in-law's baby's momma.

"Why in the world is she calling me?" thought Jo.

"Hi Dakota," greeted Jo skeptically. "What's going on?"

Jo knew something was going on, because Dakota was the master of mess, and they definitely weren't friends. Jo always did everything she could to distance herself from Dakota, so why was she calling her?

"Ooou, I found a video tape of CJ bachela party Girl. Dale recorded that shit! BAD bachela party behavior Girl!" said Dakota full of devious excitement. "I wont you to come ova TONIGHT and see this shit with me Girl, cuz dey got some thangs on this tape you gotta see. If you see what I saw, you would-na married CJ. Girl, if I can show this tape to all they ol ladies, all ov-em will break up. I was so mad when Dale gave CJ that bachela party girl. I snuck at dat hotel, and Gir---l, I saw men runnin round in dey drawls. CJ too! Even Karen ol man. And did ya hear that CJ got-a baby out there?"

"Dakota, I really don't have time for this. You may be right about everything you say and spread around town, but what does that change? Huh?" asked Jo. "Aren't you still over there with Dale? Don't you have enough business of your own to tend to? I mean with Dale beating you every other day, dragging you down the road on your back, and selling drugs. I don't appreciate you calling me on my job with this mess!"

"Not again!" said Jo, as she slammed the phone down.

"What now, Honey?" asked Ms. Melissa.

"Last week Tilly had a story to tell me about CJ's family going all around Miser talking bad about me and saying they didn't want CJ to marry me. And just now, Dakota, CJ's brother's Baby's momma called me with a bunch of mess about the bachelor party and she even said something about CJ having a baby out there somewhere. Don't they have anything else better to do?" ranted Jo.

It seemed everywhere Jo turned there was someone with some kind of story to tell her about her husband and his family. She thought

CJ would change and things would get better after they got married, but instead, it seemed things were getting worse.

Jo thought CJ would respect her more since she was his wife, but he didn't. He got much worse. He started acting as though he was entitled. One night after a very long day of work, Jo made it home to find CJ passed out drunk on the sofa. She assumed he'd been out drinking after work like most days. When he heard Jo come in, he woke up briefly.

"I thought when I married yo ass I could have sex wheneva I wanted," said CJ. "Let me fuck you in yo ass," CJ said to Jo. "Don't you want it in yo ass?"

Jo was offended, and she had no idea why CJ was talking to her that way. But like always, Jo let CJ's ugly words go into one ear and out of the other, and she blamed CJ's behavior on the alcohol.

Jo made excuses for CJ's ugly words and actions, and in time, she always forgave him.

"He does not know what he does or says when he's under the influence," Jo would say to Tamara. But deep down inside the bottom of her gut, she knew he meant every word he ever said to her when he was drunk.

"Alcohol is the greatest truth serum," said Jo.

Chapter Thirteen
Restroom

One Mardi Gras season a little over a year after Jo and CJ's wedding, CJ and his cousin Chip were driving down to New Orleans one Saturday night to see the Endymion parade and hang out in the French Quarters for a bit. Jo really didn't want to go with them, but CJ used his passive aggressive ways to convince her to go along.

"You neva wanna go with me nowhere." CJ said. "You rather be by yoself instead-a wit me."

Part of that was definitely true. Jo did not like going places with CJ, because she always felt like a lonely babysitter and designated driver without any protection. Jo really didn't want to go with them that night, but like always, she did whatever would make CJ happy.

If you enjoy a good time, New Orleans is the place to go, but during Mardi Gras time, restrooms are limited. Most places won't allow you to use their restroom unless you are a paying customer. For ladies, finding a restroom to use during Mardi Gras season is a challenge, but for men that is not case. Men just whip their things out pretty much anywhere and relieve themselves.

Jo, Chip and CJ had been out in the quarters for many hours, and Jo could not hold her pee in any longer.

"I have to use the restroom," said Jo to CJ. He heard her, but did not respond. Instead, he continued to walk through the thick crowd on Bourbon Street, drink and party. He even ducked off on a side street to drain his lizard, and there was Jo, having to pee very bad but couldn't.

"CJ, can we please find a restroom?" asked Jo. "I have to pee really bad."

Just like before, CJ heard what Jo said, but it really didn't matter. The only thing that mattered to him at that time was drinking and partying like an out of control animal.

As they continued to walk down Bourbon Street through the thick crowd, it was hard not to get separated from your group, so Chip held Jo from behind to make sure he didn't lose her. CJ was way ahead partying like a big uncontrollable kid who had never been to a playground before. He was so excited as he looked back to see where Jo and Chip were. Waving his hand beckoning for them to hurry up, he yelled over the crowd, "Come on ya'll,

let's go down there. They partyin hard down
dat street."

When Jo and Chip finally made it to CJ,
Chip went off on CJ.

"Look Dude," Chip said to CJ in a
pissed off tone. "WE AIN'T GOING NO
DAMN WHERE until I find Jo a restroom.
This is your wife, and she's been telling you she
got to use the restroom over an hour now."

"Awe man, ok then," CJ said to Chip
like a child.

"Come on Jo, come with me," said Chip,
as he grabbed her hand. "I'll find you a
restroom."

"I don't know what she's doing with
someone like you," Chip said to CJ as he
walked away guiding Jo by her hand.

A few minutes later Chip found a
restroom for Jo to use, but the doorman would
only let Jo go into the place by herself. He
wouldn't allow Chip to accompanying her, so

Chip was kind of worried about letting Jo go in that place alone. Jo had to use the restroom so bad, she didn't care.

"Jo," Chip called for her as she was rushing away to get to the restroom.

Jo looked back towards Chip, and she heard and saw him say with his mouth and hands, "I'll be standing RIGHT HERE waiting for you ok. RIGHT HERE!"

After Jo used the restroom, she felt much better, and there stood Chip, standing exactly where he said he would be standing waiting for her.

"You alright?" Chip asked her.

"Yes, I feel much better now," Jo answered. "Thank you so much for finding a restroom for me."

"Don't mention it," said Chip. "If I was you, I'd leave his ass. You deserve much better than that."

Deep inside Jo knew Chip was right, but it was a bit too late. She was already married to CJ and was serving a sentence for her very own stupidity.

As Jo and Chip walked up the street and started heading in the direction of the car, they saw CJ along the way, standing on Bourbon Street in the crowd yelling, "SHOW YOUR TITS," to a group of women standing around waving their hands in the air towards the balcony for beads. One woman did show her tits and just as promised, a man from the balcony above threw her a bead. CJ tried to intercept the bead from the woman, and when he missed, he got very angry, walked towards the sidewalk, punched the glass on a display case, and yelled, "FUCK!"

Just as he did that, shattered glass fell all over, and about ten police officers quickly appeared from nowhere, ran up behind CJ, slammed him against the wall, and put him in handcuffs.

"You coming with us," one of the officers told him.

Jo didn't know what to do. "Chip, we have to do something. We can't let them take him to jail. Especially not now during Mardi Gras time," said Jo. "Let's go talk to the police."

Chip and Jo were able to make a deal with the policeman. They gave the officer one hundred dollars cash to pay for the glass CJ broke, and they let him go. The three headed home, and neither Jo nor Chip said one word to CJ.

Jo vowed she would never go back to New Orleans with CJ again, and she didn't for many years.

Chapter Fourteen
Easter Sunday Surprise

Married life to CJ grew harder and harder with each passing minute, hour, day, and month. There was always something evil attached to CJ and his horrid family, and they never hesitated to use their devilish ways to bring someone down. Even if it meant bringing each other down too.

Every Easter Sunday CJ's family had a picnic, and they'd drink until they pass out. Jo never looked forward to spending any holidays with CJ's family, because they really didn't know the true meaning of the holidays. But most of all she despised Easter Sunday around them so much that she did everything she could do in order to avoid spending that day with them.

One particular Easter Sunday CJ begged for Jo to join him at his family's poorly put-together Easter Sunday picnic, and he invited Jo's parents too.

When CJ, Jo, her mother and father arrived at CJ's mother's house for the outside picnic, CJ's sisters were already speaking loudly with a slurred speech from their drug and alcohol usage. They were always very loud, because for some unknown reason, they always wanted their ignorance to be seen and heard.

Along with CJ's family members, the neighborhood's blueberries and strawberries were present. They usually ran around offering to help out in any way so CJ's brother Dale would pay them with drugs. Among CJ's family and the usual strawberries and blueberries, there were other people Jo didn't really know, but their faces looked quite familiar.

Jo and her parents settled down under a tree near CJ and a few other clowns, and listened as the group of fellas argued about the best way to boil crawfish, and who can do a better job. Fact is, neither of them knew what they were doing, and Jo felt sorry for the crawfish and the people who were going to eat them.

"Is that Dakota pulling up?" asked Jo's mother.

When Jo looked over towards the road, she saw Dakota, her brother-in-law Dale's woman, pulling up. Dakota stepped out of the car, and reached in the back seat to help a child, not her child, get out of a car seat, before walking over towards everyone else in the yard.

"She sure has a hot ass twitch to her walk," said one of the many clowns standing near the boiling pot.

"GIRL, DIDN'T I TELL YO ASS NOT TO COME ROUND HERE DRESS LIKE DAT!" Dale fussed at Dakota.

"I'm not studin you Dale," said Dakota. "I can dress ha-eva I wont. Ya betta check yo crack head frens. I don't have time for you anyway. I'm here ta-see CJ and Jo."

"Who dis kid you have wi-chu?" asked Dale.

"Yo nephew," said Dakota laughing. "It's bou-ta be some shit. Hey CJ! CJ!" shouted Dakota as she walked towards CJ, Jo, and Jo's parents.

"Hi Dakota," said Jo, her mother and father all in unison.

"Hey ya'll," greeted Dakota back. "Dis CJ son."

Jo was speechless and didn't know what to do or say. She just sat there staring at Dakota.

"You heard me Jo," said Dakota. "Dis CJ son. Da chile I tole you-bout."

"Jo, did you know CJ had a child with another woman?" asked her dad.

"Ya BITCH!" CJ blurted out to Dakota before Jo could answer her dad. "Who da fuck you think you are? Always startin some shit. You miserable as hell and wanna ruin otha people life. Just cuz you ain't happy, you hate to see somebody else happy. Dakota, GET YO ASS away from here!"

As CJ went on and on cursing Dakota out, Jo walked towards the little boy, who appeared to be about two years old, reached for his hand and walked him away from the ruckus. She walked him towards the ditch to look at minnows, and Jo's mother followed behind her.

"What is going on Jo?" her mother asked.

"Mom, this is not the time or place to discuss any of this. This innocent little boy should not be subjected to people like this and all of that horrible language," Jo said to her mother. "Besides Mom, I'm not sure what's going on myself."

Jo's father sat still under the tree and observed the yelling match between Dakota and CJ.

"That aint my fuckin kid," shouted CJ to everyone standing by watching. "Dale, you betta get yo crazy ass woman."

"Call me crazy all you wont CJ. Dats yo child," shouted Dakota. "Crazy! I GOT YO crazy. ALL ya'll fuckin crazy! All ya'll and yo momma too. Where da kid went?" asked Dakota as she looked around for who was supposed to be CJ's illegitimate child.

"Jo, I'm sorry fa dis but you had to know," said Dakota.

"I appreciate you telling me something you think I have to know. But Dakota! This way! Why did you have to do it this way?" asked Jo. "This innocent little boy should not have been subjected to that. What do you or anyone have to gain from the mess you started here today? There isn't any excuse for what you did."

"CJ can say dis ain't his kid, but he a fuckin liar," said Dakota. "Look-a dis lil boy. Don't he look like CJ? CJ know dis kid his. He wont claim it cuz da boy momma didn't name the baby afta him."

"Dakota, who is the baby's mother?" asked Jo.

"My fren Madalene," answered Dakota.

"I know Madalene. Doesn't she have other kids?" asked Jo.

"Yeah!" replied Dakota. "She got three sons with two otha baby daddies. Right na she don't have ha kids cuz da office of child service or whateva took ha kids from ha."

"Where is Madalene now?" asked Jo.

"Madalene my fren and all, but she-a crack head. She-a ho too," said Dakota. "How-ya think CJ know ha? She wonted dope from Dale. Nobody wont ha but yo no good sneaky ass husband CJ."

"Yes Dakota, but where is she now? Why do you have her child?" asked Jo, again.

"Right na Madalene in da hospital goin dru rehab. Ha momma raisin dis one, and she havin-a hard time cuz she ain't well ha-self. CJ need ta step up and be a daddy to dis boy."

After Dakota took the child away, Jo and her parents left.

"I told her ass not to mess with that nigga," said Jo's dad to her mom.

When Jo made it home, she climbed into bed and went to sleep. Nothing no one could say to her would make her feel better or any less stupid than she'd been feeling since the moment she had taken CJ into her life.

Chapter Fifteen
Wife's Duty

CJ never took full responsibility for his actions. He always blamed everyone else, or had some kind of ridiculous excuse for what he did. This time Dakota was the blame for Jo wanting to pack up his bags and send him back to his mother's house across the tracks.

"CJ, is that little boy your kid?" asked Jo.

Smiling from ear to ear, with that unattractive shit eating Cheshire no lips smile of his, CJ said nothing, but shook his head yes.

"When were you planning to tell me?" asked Jo.

"Jo, you ain't need to know that," said CJ, still grinning from ear to ear.

"WHY IN THE HELL ARE YOU SMILLING? You act like you don't have the common sense babies are born with," said Jo.

"It aint non-a-ya bizness," said CJ.

"None of my business," Jo thought.

Jo was hurt deeply when she'd learned that another woman had given birth to CJ's child a few months before she married him. On the other hand, being hurt by CJ wasn't anything new. Since CJ told Jo his illegitimate son wasn't any of her business, that is exactly how she left it. She didn't ask any more questions, until the day CJ started begging her to have kids for him.

"You know I don't want to have any kids, and why do you want a kid with me when you already have one you don't acknowledge or take care of?" asked Jo.

"You my wife," replied CJ. "If we have a kid it'll make us stronga."

"Just go and be stronger with Madalene. She's your baby's momma. Did having a kid with her make ya'll stronger?" asked Jo sarcastically.

"Jo, I don't like Madalene. I neva did. I just fooled with ha cuz it seem like you don't wont me," said CJ. "Plus she a freak. She give up ass anytime I wont it."

As the years went by, Jo kept trudging through life in an unhappy state. She continued to bear with CJ's neglect and passive aggressiveness by looking past it. The way Jo was raised, it was unacceptable to divorce, so no matter what CJ did to her, it was her duty to take it, and do whatever she needed to do to please her husband.

Four years into her marriage to CJ, and after several trips to the fertility doctor, Jo gave birth to their first daughter, Isabella. CJ was a bit disappointed when Isabella was born, because he was hoping for a son to name after himself; a junior.

CJ was just the kind of father Jo expected him to be. Not much of a dad at all. It was all about the front for CJ. Look at my wife. Look at my daughter. We so happy.

Those are the things he liked to project to others, but in actuality, his wife was miserable as hell, because he was a horrible husband and father.

Jo worked day in and day out to keep a good household. She kept up with the bills, the cleaning, cooking, and Isabella. In time, Jo was able to go back to work at UPS, and things were going just fine for her and Isabella. Jo figured the best way for her to get by was to ignore CJ and all of his foolishness as much as she could.

Her number one priority was taking care of Isabella.

In time, CJ finally figured out that Jo could care less about him, and that didn't sit well with him at all.

"I don't have time to worry about your grown ass," said Jo to CJ. "I have Isabella to take care of. You can go away, drink, and party with your people. Isabella and I will be just fine. I'll make sure of that. Like always."

"I wanna be in you and Isabella life Jo," said CJ.

"We've always been here CJ. If you really wanted that, you wouldn't be the way you are," said Jo.

Four years later, Jo gave birth to her and CJ's second child; another daughter whom she named Jaylynn. After giving birth to Jaylynn, Jo decided that would be her last child, even though CJ wanted her to have three kids for him. Jo felt two children were more than enough for her; especially after all the trouble she had conceiving, carrying, and giving birth to them.

Just as before, CJ was upset because Jo did not give birth to a son for him. He blamed Jo, and got worse than he'd ever been.

Chapter Sixteen
No More Tinted Glasses

So desperate for a happy marriage and family, Jo continued making excuses for CJ's behavior.

"Maybe he really does love us, but just doesn't know how to show it. His mother or sisters definitely weren't any kind of role models," she'd say.

Jo believed that lie and continued to make excuses for many years until Tiffany started coming around to all of their family gatherings.

Tiffany was a woman CJ had known for many years before Jo ever entered his life. She was related to some of CJ's cousins, and it seemed every time Jo and CJ would host a family gathering, Tiffany would come. No matter how much time had passed by, Jo could never forget two of the family events that Tiffany attended.

One Evening Jo and CJ hosted a Christmas Eve dinner at their home, and Tiffany was there. The house was pretty loud as it always was when CJ and his family were around. For some reason, CJ, his mom and siblings were always fighting to be center of attention, but CJ always won. He was the loudest and funniest. He always had a story to tell about himself of course, and in every story he'd made a complete ass of himself one way or another. That evening CJ told story after story, and the people who were listening to him laughed and laughed. On the other hand, Jo and her family didn't bother to listen to his stories anymore because they'd heard them thousands of times before. It was always the same thing with CJ and his family, so most mature people present would tune out their rambunctious behavior.

As time went by that evening the noise level in the house subsided a little, and CJ's older sister stated loudly, "It got quiet in here all of a sudden."

Everyone looked around and his other sister Jackie said, "It's cuz CJ and Tiffany ain't here no mo."

"Where dey went?" asked Pam.

"I don't know," answered Jackie.

Jo rarely ever paid attention to anything they said, but she did hear when his two heartless sisters said that, because they said it in a way to make sure Jo heard them.

For one moment, Jo felt embarrassed, because then everyone there knew that her husband was off with another woman. On the other hand, Jo brushed it off and thought, "Oh well. What's new? CJ is always making an ass of me one way or another."

About an hour later, CJ and Tiffany came back into the house.

"Where ya'll been?" asked Pam.

"Yeah! Where ya'll been. You two been gone a long time," agreed Jackie.

Neither CJ nor Tiffany said a word. CJ just stood there smiling his ugly lipless and sneaky smile like he always did, and Tiffany just smiled at CJ without saying a word. Jo took note, and coached herself not to let it bother her.

Towards the end of the night, Jo went into her office which was off of the master suite in her house. Just as she walked into the office, there was CJ and Tiffany coming out of her master bathroom together. When CJ saw Jo, he looked like a deer in headlights.

"Uh, Uh," CJ said as he was fighting to get other words to come out of his mouth. "She had to use the bathroom and I didn't want ha to wait for da otha two."

"No problem," said Jo, as she proceeded to do what she went into her office to do.

CJ and Tiffany went back among the party population, and Jo quickly replayed in her head what she'd just witnessed.

"Now why would they be coming out of the bathroom together?" Jo thought. "And why couldn't she use the other two bathrooms like everyone else? It was ok for his seventy-five year old aunt to wait for one of the other bathrooms, but it wasn't ok for Tiffany to wait."

Jo pushed that in the back of her mind too. Just like she did everything else CJ had done. That was until Miss Tiffany showed up at a fourth of July picnic at Jo's parents' house.

Just like always, CJ was loud as ever visiting with everyone, until Tiffany arrived of course. When she arrived, no one else existed to CJ. Not even his daughters. All of his attention went towards Tiffany. What Tiffany wanted to drink, CJ got. Whatever Tiffany wanted to eat, he made sure he made a plate with her foods of choice on it.

That day Jo took a few minutes to observe CJ's attentive behavior towards Tiffany, and she wasn't the only person to notice what was going on.

"Mom," said Isabella to Jo. "Who is that woman daddy talking to? I went over to ask him something and he told me to go away. Ever since that woman been here, he's been talking to her. That's not right Mom."

"It's ok Honey," said Jo to her older daughter. "She's just a woman he knows since they were kids."

"Well he should talk to other people too. Not just her," said Isabella.

The day continued to pass by, and Jo was quite the hostess like always. She was very busy serving guests and getting things they wanted. Many times she had to go inside to get items to replenish on the picnic tables. During one of her many trips inside, where no one was, there she saw CJ and Tiffany coming out of the hallway where the bathroom was in her parents' house. Just like before, CJ was rather speechless, and Jo could tell he was trying to think of something to say.

"Uh, Uh," CJ said as he grinned. "Tiffany didn't know where da bathroom was so I came with ha."

"Not a problem," Jo said as she got what she needed and went back outside.

"My mother's house isn't large at all," Jo thought. "And there are a lot of people here. Why is he the only one who could show Tiffany the bathroom?"

About an hour later, Jo caught CJ in her parents' house waiting on Tiffany to come out of the bathroom again, but that time, CJ didn't say a word. "I guess she forgot where the bathroom was huh?" asked Jo sarcastically and all knowing.

Seeing how CJ was with Tiffany didn't even upset Jo. It only confirmed what she'd known since the beginning. CJ did not love her, and she was right about actions speaking louder than words.

The excuse about CJ not knowing how to love or show love was then null and void. He had no problem showing love or expressing love when he had love to show. He knew how to treat a woman after all. When he cared about them that is. It was obvious that CJ cared about Tiffany. To Jo, he cared more about Tiffany than he'd ever cared about her or their daughters.

Jo never forgot the night she was in New Orleans with CJ and Chip during Mardi Gras season. The night she had to use the restroom so bad and CJ didn't even bother to help her, his very own wife, find one. Not even in that dangerous and crowded place. But there he was, escorting a woman who was not his wife, to the restroom in a safe home, and also waiting for her to come out.

CJ did many bad things to Jo throughout the years, but none of them resonated within her like the bathroom incidents.

Chapter Seventeen
Candy

The years seemed to fly by so fast and the girls grew and grew. Before Jo could blink an eye, she already had two grown daughters. One was already out of high school and the other was just beginning high school. Jo and CJ's marriage never got any better, because CJ was the same as he'd always been, and Jo quit caring. She busied herself with work as much as she could, and developed a personal life since the girls weren't babies anymore.

Jo didn't return back to UPS after Jaylynn was born. Instead, she started her very own interior decorating firm in Miser. She first began working out of her house, and in no time, business increased, and space at home decreased. Since business was booming, and finances weren't an issue anymore, Jo rented out office and storage space in town, hired a few designers, and with that, JoJo's Interior Design Firm became one of the most sought out firms in the south.

One evening Jo was in the kitchen preparing dinner, and her younger daughter Jaylynn was hanging out telling her all about her day at school. Jaylynn spoke a lot about a girl named Ann. Ann was a new student in Jaylynn's school and she also lived next door. It seemed as though Jaylynn and Ann were forming a close relationship, because the two girls were always on the phone with one another, and Ann invited Jaylynn to come over and hang out at her house.

Even though Ann lived right next door, Jo was reluctant to allow Jaylynn to go over to her house, because Ann's mother was rarely ever home. Ann was home alone pretty often, and Jo observed teenage boys going in and out of that house. Boys are the only thing most girls that age think about, and based on Jaylynn's rambling, Ann's hormones were raging.

"Jaylynn, before I allow you to go over to Ann's house, I'd like to meet her mother first," said Jo.

"Why mom!" asked Jaylynn. "You are always trying to watch me."

"It's for your own good Jaylynn. It's my job to protect you," said Jo.

Jaylynn called Ann on the phone.

"Ann, my mom said I can come over to your house, but she want to meet your mom first. Is she home now?" asked Jaylynn.

Ann's mother was home at that time, so Jo walked outside to the side of her house, and

met Candy Minnow, Ann's mom. The two
ladies greeted each other and chatted for a long
while about themselves and their daughters.
Candy was overly friendly, and extremely open,
but Jo being the private type of person she was,
did most of the listening.

Candy was a single mother, divorced
with two daughters at home, and one older
daughter living away. Candy was new to
Miser, and she worked as an assistant to a
wealthy business owner in Biloxi, Mississippi.
She was originally from New Orleans,
Louisiana, and she moved from there a few
years before, after going through a bitter divorce
and custody battle with her ex-husband.

During the ladies' lengthy conversation,
Jo learned that Candy did not only work as her
boss' assistant, she was also his mistress, and he
was paying her rent so she could live in a decent
neighborhood in a decent school district. The
court system made Candy promise to provide

adequate housing for her daughters, as well as enroll them in a good school district. If Candy could not provide those two things for her daughters, she would lose them to their father again. Candy was not able to provide those things on her salary alone; therefore, she turned to selling herself for the things she needed. It's the same as what most people call prostitution.

"My boss wants what's best for my daughters and me, so he pays my rent just so Ann and my other daughter can go to a better school," said Candy.

"And what do you have to do for your boss in return?" asked Jo.

"Gi--rl, you know," giggled Candy.

"Oh! Don't get it confused. I DON'T know. I can only assume," replied Jo.

"Put it this way Gi---rl" said Candy. "He takes care of my needs and I take care of his."

"What about the man's wife?" asked Jo. "Don't you ever think about her? Do you think what you and her husband are doing is right?"

"I don't care about his wife. As long as he pays my bills, Girl," said Candy. "If it wasn't for him, I couldn't afford to pay the rent for this nice house. Between him and the child support I get from these girls' daddy, that's the only way I am making it. The little money I make working don't pay much."

Just as the ladies stood outside talking, CJ pulled into the driveway and got out of his truck. "Hello," he said as he waved and walked indoors.

"Who is that?" asked Candy.

"That's my husband, CJ," answered Jo.

"Is THAT your husband? I saw him earlier today," said Candy.

"Oh really. Where?" asked Jo.

"He came on my job in Biloxi today. He was there dropping off some packages for my boss, Mr. Harwell," said Candy.

"Mr. Harwell is your boss? The Mr. Harwell who owns the Harwell high rise buildings?" asked Jo.

"Yes, how do you know Mr. Harwell?" asked Candy.

"He is one of my clients," answered Jo. "I own my own interior design firm, and Mr. Harwell hired me to design his newest building in Bilioxi. CJ, my husband was there today delivering some items that my designers need in order to complete the job."

"Girl, oh my God! Gir---l, I'm so crazy. You are Jo! Jo! The owner of Jo's Interior Decorating Firm."

"Yes I am," replied Jo.

"It's a small world," said Candy.

"Yes, it sure is," agreed Jo.

"Jo, don't trust your husband," said Candy, abruptly.

Looking at Candy in a questionable way, Jo asked, "Why do you say that?"

"I told you he came into the office today. He was flirting with me Girl. He was flirting so hard, that I didn't think he was married. Now here he is. Your husband, and my neighbor too," said Candy.

"Candy, don't mistake his friendliness for flirting. That's just the way CJ is," said Jo.

"Well the way he was coming on to me today wasn't just friendliness," replied Candy.

Jo knew Candy was right, but she didn't spend much time worrying about CJ's dirty doings anymore.

Later that night when Jo was cleaning up the kitchen after dinner, CJ asked her, "What you doin out there talkin to dat bitch?"

"Why are you calling her out of her name?" asked Jo.

"I saw ha today when I made dose deliveries fa-ya. Dat bitch barely spoke to me," said CJ. "She think she all that with ha ova made up ass. And I'm willing to bet she fuckin Mr. Harwell."

"She's a woman on hard times CJ. Don't judge," said Jo.

"Hard time my ass. If dat bitch is fuckin Mr. Harwell like I know she is," said CJ, "what da fuck that otha dude at ha house all da time fa?"

"I see you've been paying a lot of attention to her," said Jo. "Why haven't you mentioned her before?"

CJ had no answer for that question. Instead, he turned the attention away from himself and onto Jo, just like a passive aggressive person does when they are questioned.

"Jo, I'm so glad you not a woman like dat. You don't needa wear all dat shit on yo face to look good. Dat bitch is all made up, and I bet if she take dat shit off, she ugly as fuck. And got nerve to be stuck up an think she all dat," said CJ.

Chapter Eighteen
Any Reason to Party

CJ continued to work and spend all of his money on partying. Jo continued to run her business, the household, pay bills, and clean up CJ's financial messes. One weekend CJ's trifling family was giving another party.

"Jo, I need-a hundred fiddy dolla to buy a keg for da pardee at my momma dis weekend," said CJ.

"What party?" asked Jo.

"Dey havin a get tagetha Sunday cuz Dale got to turn himself in at da jail house Monday," said CJ.

"That is the most ridiculous thing I have ever heard of," said Jo. "You and your people will find any reason to party. Instead of sending him off with a party, you all need to be praying and asking for forgiveness and protection," said Jo. "I refuse to have one hundred fifty dollars of my hard earned money spent on such foolishness. Your momma and sisters knew exactly what Dale was doing all that time, and now they have the audacity to cry some damn tears because he's going off to prison. Hell, if I was the judge, I'd drag your momma and sisters to prison with Dale too," ranted Jo. "All your momma did was sit her ass back there and enable Dale to sell dope. What kind of momma sit on her ass and allow her son to live in her house and sell dope out of it. And them sorry ass sisters of yours! They helped him sling dope from the window one night and bragged all around town about it. Their dumb asses said, 'Dale tode us he made his money for the night,

129

so whatever we sell we could keep.' What kind of shit is that? And you want me to give you money. Hell no! What happened to all that dope money?"

"Jo, you betta give me dat money," said CJ.

"I will not give you shit. I'm tired of YOU and your NO GOOD ass family. Hell no! All they've ever done was run around town and talk about me because I was trying to better us," said Jo.

"Dat's my family ova there across them tracks Jo, and they needa keg for da pardee. I'm gettin it with money from our account. Just so you know," said CJ.

"I thought we were your family here. I'm your wife and these two girls are your daughters," said Jo.

CJ looked at Jo without one ounce of confusion as he pointed in the direction of the tracks and said, "Dat's MY family ova there. DEY MY FAMILY," said CJ.

"What about your daughters?" asked Jo.

"MY FAMILY is ova there across the tracks," repeated CJ.

From that point on, Jo knew without a shadow of a doubt exactly where she stood and what she and her daughters meant to CJ. The following Monday, Jo went to the credit union and opened up an account in just her name. She made arrangements for her money to go directly to that private bank account that CJ didn't have access to. Jo refused to continue to go on and allow CJ to waste all of her hard earned money, and she was tired of always cleaning up his financial messes.

There were times when Jo had to travel out of state for jobs. Some of those times, Jo was able to take the girls with her, but other times she was not. Fortunately, Jo's mother had been in remission and physically healthy since her granddaughters entered the world, so she'd been around a lot to help Jo with the girls. Sometimes Jo's mother was not able to help, but that didn't stop Jo.

"CJ, these girls are your daughters too, so it's high time you get off of your ass and do your part. I am going off making money so we can live without financial struggles like before," said Jo. "The least you can do is BE here for your daughters. Start being a daddy to them. At least while I go off to work."

Jo's daughters were growing, her business had grown, and so had her self-esteem. Since she'd begun working for herself, she was no longer a weak little wife she'd been for years.

Jo had long before given up on CJ, so she could care less what he did. As long as he was there for the girls when she couldn't be, was all that mattered to Jo.

Jo felt blessed to have two beautiful daughters, a nice house, reliable vehicles, a booming business, and good health, but she still felt very lonely and unhappy most of the time. She seemed to have had it all, but still did not have what she needed most. Love.

Jo continued to busy herself with work, and she prayed that someday God would send her love. Jo had always known CJ did not love her. As much as he said, "Jo, I'm mad about you," that didn't mean a thing to her.

"CJ I know you don't love me, and it's really ok," Jo would say.

"Girl, you crazy. If only you knew. I love you more than anything else in this world," said CJ. "I'm mad about you."

"Actions speak louder than words," Jo would always say. "And your actions speak volumes."

Chapter Nineteen
Penance

CJ was Jo's husband and he didn't love her the way a husband should love a wife. Steve Harvey says, "When a man loves a woman, he will protect her, profess his love for her, and provide for her."

CJ never did any of those three things for Jo. On the other hand, Jo did see him do more than one of those things for Tiffany. He provided for her and even protected her when he didn't need to.

From day one, Jo regretted marrying CJ, and she prayed with all she had that God would release her from all the hurt he brought into her life.

"Tamara, sometimes I pray for CJ not to come home. I know that is not right, but that is how I feel," said Jo.

"Divorce his ass!" said Tamara.

"I can't do that," said Jo. "I married him. I made that choice, so it's my job to suffer the consequences of my wrong decision."

As Jo continued through each day, she looked and prayed for solutions to her CJ problems, and little by little, the burden of having CJ began to lift off of her chest. Jo realized it was her job to take control of her life, and to be a strong role model for her daughters. Then is when Jo began to look at her life as her own, and she decided to take her life from CJ, and hold on to it for herself and God.

From that point on, Jo wiped CJ and his horrible family from her mind. She began to live as though they didn't exist. She worked when she wanted to, spent time with her parents and daughters when she wanted or needed to, and she even started taking time for herself. Besides traveling just for business, Jo began to travel for leisure as well. She traveled all over, and took as many vacations as she could. Some she took with her daughters, some CJ would tag along, and other vacations she took alone. Sometimes when Jo went on vacations alone, she felt like Stella in Terry McMillan's novel, *How Stella Got her Groove Back.* Many eligible bachelors approached and pursued Jo, and that rejuvenated her in ways she'd never imagined. Jo's self-esteem and self-worth began to increase, and that helped her grow into womanhood like never before.

One summer Jo and Jaylynn were going on a special mother daughter vacation to Disney Land, and Jaylynn wanted to invite her friend and neighbor, Ann, to go along. When Jo went over to speak with Ann's mother Candy about their summer trip, Candy kept hinting around about wanting to go too.

"I'd really like to go on the mother daughter trip with you and the girls, but I really don't have the money," said Candy. "You are such a good mother Jo, to plan mother daughter time and invite my daughter too. I wish I could go."

Jo felt sorry for Candy, and since she considered that vacation to be a mother daughter vacation, she extended the invitation to Candy, and of course Candy happily accepted the mostly all-expense paid vacation.

Jo, her daughter Jaylynn, Candy, and her daughter Ann went on a long and adventurous road trip to California from Mississippi and back. The only thing Candy had to provide was spending money for herself and her daughter Ann. Jo paid for transportation, all hotel expenses, and even some of their entertainment and meals. The four had a great time together, and that gave Jo time to get to know Candy a little more.

After spending nearly two weeks around Candy, Jo learned that Candy was not a person she wanted too close around her life.

"Watch this woman," said the still small voice in Jo's gut.

Chapter Twenty
Let's Go Speak

Upon the ladies return from their two week west coast vacation, they all went back to their normal routines. When CJ found out Candy joined Jo and Jaylynn on their mother daughter vacation, he was greatly disturbed.

"Why you invite ha to go with y'all?" asked CJ.

"Jaylynn wanted Ann to come, so I invited Candy too since it was a mother daughter vacation," said Jo.

"Well, I tode ya I don't like dat stuck up bitch," said CJ.

"Her coming with me has nothing to do with you CJ," said Jo.

Jo felt it was rather strange for CJ to be talking that way about Candy, because if he didn't like her, he sure had a funny way of showing his dislike in front of Candy's face.

Whenever CJ, Jo and their younger daughter Jaylynn would go to Sunday morning mass, they'd sometimes see Candy and her daughters. When CJ saw Candy at church, an uncontrollable excitement came over him.

"Look at Candy ya'll," he'd say. "Let's go ova there an speak."

When Jo wasn't rushing over to say hello to Candy, CJ grew impatient, and he'd leave Jo and Jaylynn to go talk to Candy himself. To Candy's face, CJ flirted and Candy flirted right back. They flirted with each other right in front of Jo, but Jo could care less. And when they'd finally part from Candy, CJ wouldn't stop talking about her. He'd go on and on.

"Candy got it goin on," CJ would say. "She drives a nice car and all."

"If you say so," replied Jo. "For someone who doesn't like Candy, you sure do flirt with her a lot, and she knows it."

"Dat's a fuckin lie," said CJ. "I don't flirt with dat bitch. She think everybody like ha ass, so I tease her. Make ha think I want ha. I can't stand women like ha. I was bein nice ta-ha cuz aint ya'll friens now? Ya'll went on vacation togetha and all."

"I'm nice to her CJ, because that's how I am," said Jo.

"She alright," said CJ.

"You're such a hypocrite," Jo said. "One minute you talk bad about the woman, and now you're here trying to convince me to be her friend. I know you lack decency, but I also know she lacks decency as a woman too."

"Ha-ya gonna say dat about ha?" asked CJ.

"First CJ, I don't have to answer to a hypocrite. You just called the woman a bitch a few minutes ago, and now you are defending her. A woman you really don't know. Getting back to what I was saying. She lacks decency and self-respect, because any woman who has self-respect or common decency would not entertain or flirt with another woman's husband; especially when his wife is standing right there. And to top it all off, Candy refers to me as her friend."

"You're too hard on da woman Jo," said CJ.

"No, I'm not stupid anymore CJ," replied Jo.

Candy tried to contact Jo nearly every day. Whenever she saw Jo pulling up in the driveway, she'd run over. Sometimes she'd walk inside with Jo and make herself at home.

All Candy did was talk talk talk. She talked so much, about so many different people, that she got on Jo's nerves. Candy was what some call a name dropper. She thought knowing many different people made her somebody. She was always trying to impress someone by saying who she knew.

"Girl, you know so and so. You know so and so's sister, mother, brother. That lady who works at the post office. Yeah Girl! We met for coffee the other day," Candy would say.

Candy was always inviting Jo to meet her at Starbucks, but Jo declined most of the times. Meeting Candy one time at Starbucks was enough to let Jo know that she never wanted to do that again. Jo told Candy time and time again that she did not drink coffee or caffeinated products, but Candy didn't have enough sense to know not to continue to invite Jo to Starbucks?

Candy was very much self-centered and she was always on the phone talking to someone, about someone who knows someone or whatever, and if she wasn't talking to someone on the phone, she was on Messbook logging her every move, and posting pictures of herself just like teenage girls do.

Jo called Facebook Messbook, and Candy spent her life on Messbook.

Most people who met Candy described her as a woman who was starving for attention, and she loved to get it from men. Most times she was seen giggling and talking to men, seeking her next victim.

When Tamara and Uncle Charlie was at Jo's house one Christmas Eve, Candy was there too, and Uncle Charlie said Candy was too much for him. She'd made him feel uncomfortable that night, because he said she was too damn flirtatious.

Over time, Jo's daughter Jaylynn didn't want to talk to or spend time with Candy's daughter Ann anymore.

"What is going on Jaylynn? Ann is always calling for you. Why are you so ugly to her?" asked Jo.

"Mom, you just don't know," replied Jaylynn.

"Candy wants you to come over and celebrate Ann's birthday with them. I think that's the least you can do Jaylynn," said Jo.

"NO! You can't make me go!" said Jaylynn.

"What happened Jaylynn?" asked Jo

"They disgusting," said Jaylynn. "Ann and Candy are whores," said Jaylynn.

"What did they do?" asked Jo, "And stop using that language," she added.

"Nothing Mom! Nothing! Just know I'm never going over there again," yelled Jaylynn.

Chapter Twenty-One
Numb

Less than a year after the mother daughter California vacation, Candy and her daughters had to move out of the house that was next door to Jo and CJ. Mr. Harwell found out about Candy being with other men, so he fired her and cut off financial support. On top of that, Candy's second daughter made eighteen and graduated from high school, so her Candy's support check from her ex-husband decreased to half of what she was used to receiving. No more sugar daddy and not as much child support meant Candy had to downsize.

Since CJ had a truck, he offered to help
Candy move her furniture to the smaller
apartment she was moving into across town.
While CJ was helping Candy move, he and
Candy spoke about Jaylynn not wanting to be
friends with Ann anymore.

"What dat girl do to you Jaylynn?" CJ
asked his daughter. "She wont you-ta come ova
to da apartment to swim wit-ha. What's da
harm in dat?"

"Dad, you can like them if you want to,
but I don't have to and you can't make me,"
said Jaylynn.

"Jo, do you know what's goin own wit-
dat?" asked CJ.

"CJ, they are high school teenagers, and
I refuse to get involved in their drama,"
answered Jo. "If Jaylynn doesn't want to be
friends with Ann anymore, there isn't anything
we can do about it. Frankly, based on some

things I've seen around here and on vacation, I don't blame Jaylynn."

"Candy wanted me-ta bring Jaylynn ova there to swim. Jaylynn like-ta swim, so I thought it wouldn't be a problem," said CJ.

"Dad, don't play dumb," said Jaylynn.

"Jaylynn, don't talk to your dad that way," insisted Jo.

"Mom, why are you always taking up for him? You are the last person who need to do that. Especially the way he is with you," scoffed Jaylynn.

"What are you talking about young lady?" asked Jo.

"Jo, you know Jaylynn crazy and always startin some kinda mess. She just like my sista. Her Auntie Pam," teased CJ.

"I can't stand yo people, and I don't like when you tell me I am like them. Especially that sister of yours. I wish I can change my last name from Sims. I hate being a Sims," said Jaylynn to her dad as he walked out of the door.

"Maybe when you get older, you can check into changing your last name if you hate it that much," said Jo. "Honestly, I don't blame you. When I married your dad, the last thing I wanted to do was take on his terrible last name, but he insisted."

"Mom, every time Dad came to pick me up from Candy's place, he stayed a very long time doing a little more than talking to Candy," said Jaylynn.

"Yes, I know you two would come home rather late," Jo agreed.

"Him and Candy be flirting with each other, and one time when Ann and I walked into the kitchen, I could swear I saw them two kissing, but when I asked him about it, he told me I was crazy and seeing things. And Ann was all happy talking about me and her was going to be sisters. All I could do was think about you, and tears started rolling down my face."

"You're not crazy honey, and you probably did see what you think you saw," said Jo to her daughter. "When did that happen honey?"

"It happened about six months after Dad helped her move where she lives now. You not mad, Mom?" asked Jaylynn.

"Honey, your dad has done me so much wrong through the years, that I am numb to the things he does to me these days," said Jo.

Chapter Twenty-Two
Enough

Jo didn't like what her daughter told her. It was one thing for CJ to hurt her, but for him to expose her daughter to his baneful ways was another.

Anger took over Jo to the point that she felt like she could really hurt someone. She didn't know who she wanted to hurt more. Candy or CJ. If Jo reacted while she was infuriated, she would hurt someone to the point of no return, and she didn't want to do that because she feared jail.

Instead, Jo chose to stay calm for many days, and during that time, she went apartment hunting. After she secured an apartment, she secretly and quietly began to pack in a way that CJ wouldn't notice.

CJ's job was sending him out of town for a few weeks for work, so the Sunday night before the Monday morning he was scheduled to leave, Jo stuck a note inside of his suitcase, informing him of her plans to move out of their marital home while he was away.

Jo thought CJ would get the letter after he left, but she was wrong. He had to go into his suitcase that morning for something, and when he did, he found the letter she'd placed in there the night before. Around 5:30 that Monday morning, CJ showed up on the side of Jo's bed balling his eyes out.

"Why are you leaving me?" he asked. "Please don't give up on me."

At that point in time, Jo had enough of CJ, and there was not one morsel of feeling left inside of her for him. CJ could have cried himself to the point of dehydration, and Jo wouldn't even bother get him a glass of water.

Jo made it quite clear to CJ how she felt, but he still continued to beg her to come back to him. CJ hadn't shown any ounce of manhood to Jo in over a twenty year time span, but all of a sudden, it seemed he'd found a little. He did everything in his will power to shower Jo and coax her back, but none of it worked. Jo moved on with her life by filing for divorce, and when CJ was served with divorce papers, he cried and cried again for weeks. When the court date came for the divorce to be finalized, he cried even harder, but that still did not stop him from trying to get Jo back.

"How could you give up on me?" CJ consistently asked Jo.

"What's wrong with you women? None of ya'll wont a decent man," said CJ. "And why you have to go and break my family up?"

"Please tell me you don't fancy yourself a decent man," said Jo. "If you are what people consider to be decent, then no, I don't want a decent man."

"Why you always hurt my feelings? Always gotta say somethin to beat me down," said CJ.

"I state facts CJ," said Jo. "If the shoe fits!"

"Ima good man. I take care a-mine," said CJ.

"You obviously don't know what a decent man is," said Jo. "And you don't have any family here. Remember? YOUR FAMILY lives across the tracks."

"Na ya gonna hole somethin I said when I was drunk ova my head," said CJ.

154

"YOU said it. The girls and I aren't your family," said Jo. "So go run along across the tracks back to YOUR family."

"I wont you. I love you. If only you can climb inside my body and see how I feel about you," pleaded CJ.

"How can you stand here and beg me to be with you when you've been seeing Candy all along?" asked Jo. "And even if you weren't seeing Candy, I still don't want your dirty ass."

"What you talkin 'bout? I'm not seein Candy. I told ya I don't like dat bitch. She think she all dat. Whoever tode you dat is a lie," said CJ.

"YOU ARE A LIAR CJ. A BIG FAKE. Not man enough to tell the truth," said Jo. "Just admit it CJ. You and Candy are seeing one another, and here you are begging me back."

"I been talkin to Candy on the phone. That's it! Come on Jo. If you come back to me, I'll quit talkin to ha," said CJ. "I don't love ha.

155

YOU who I love. My heart will always belong to you. No matter what."

"CJ, please stop begging me," said Jo. "I already don't have any respect for you, and the more you beg, I respect you that much less."

"Candy been worrying and wondering what you might think of her if you found out about us," said CJ.

"Tell Candy there is no need to wonder. If she is woman enough, have her call or come see me like she used to do. Invite me to Starbucks," Jo said as she laughed. "I'll be more than happy to share my thoughts about her to her face. But since she is a coward and an embarrass piece of shit, I know she is hoping she'll never see me again. When you TALK to her the next time, please give her this message."

Even though Jo knew CJ was too big of a passive aggressive coward to deliver the messages she was sending for Candy, she still gave him an earful of her thoughts to stew on.

If CJ didn't tell Candy what she had to say, Jo still got peace in knowing that CJ himself knew exactly what she thought.

"First," said Jo. "Tell Candy she got what I didn't want. Second. The fact that she is with you shows that she lacks class, morals, and self-respect. Third. I know what you are, so I don't envy her."

"Stop it Jo!" said CJ. "Stop it and just come back to me! I wanna be with YOU! Not ha, but YOU! You won't go anywhere or do anything with me," said CJ. "Sometimes I just want somebody to party with."

"CJ, I don't want you anywhere near me. The last time I invited you to spend the holidays away with my family, you got so damn drunk that you didn't even know you were pissing in the corner of a bedroom," said Jo. "As much as I despise Candy's no good ass, I feel sorry for her at the same time."

"Why you feel sorry fa ha?" asked CJ.

157

"I feel sorry for her because here you are begging to be with me, and I know when you are with her, you are wishing you were with me," said Jo.

"Yes," CJ said crying. "I do! So PLEASE. I'm beggin you Jo. Come back to me. PLEASE! Don't give up on me."

"You obviously don't know what it means to give up CJ." said Jo. "I don't think it is considered giving up after spending over twenty years working on something. Did you really think I'd continue to stand by and keep allowing you to make an ass of me for twenty more years? Everybody has a breaking point, and getting away from you and your atrocious family was the best thing I ever did," ranted Jo.

"If you were the last man on this earth, I still wouldn't be with you," said Jo. "You and Candy are two decorated pieces of trash who deserve one another. A perfect fairy tale ya'll make."

In a very calm manner Jo said, "Once upon a time there was a female piece of trash named Candy, and male piece of trash named CJ. After spending most of their lives manipulating others, Candy and CJ crossed paths at the bottom of a dumpster. They both lacked common sense and decency, and enjoyed stooping low down quite often. Partying was both of their favorite past time, and they spent a lot of time attending social functions in other dumpsters with trash just like themselves."

As Jo turned towards her future, she glanced back at CJ with a smile on her face and peace in her heart and said, "CJ, you and Candy are what I call **The True Essence of Evil.**"

Also by Açil Pichon

Evil In Front of You
Book One of the Stories of Jo Series

MORE BOOKS TO COME
Evil's Last Look
Book Three of the Stories of Jo Series

Visit us at: **www.acilpichon.com**

Printed in the United States of America